myth ADVENTURES one

by Robert Asprin and Phil Foglio
Art by Phil Foglio
Colors by Cecelia Cosentini and Phil Foglio • Inks by Tim Sale
Edited by Kay Reynolds and Richard Pini

Starblaze Graphics • The Donning Company/Publishers
Norfolk/Virginia Beach 1985

Myth Adventures One contains the story found in issues one through four of the black and white *Myth Adventures* magazine published by WaRP Graphics.

Myth Adventures One is one of many graphic novels published by The Donning Company/Publishers. For a complete listing of our titles, please write to the address below.

The Donning Company/Publishers
5659 Virginia Beach Boulevard
Norfolk, Virginia 23502

10 9 8 7 6 5 4 3 2 1

Library of Congress Cataloging-in-Publication Data:

Foglio, Phil
    Myth adventures one.
    I. Reynolds, Kay, 1951-   . II. Pini, Richard. III. Asprin, Robert. Another fine myth. IV. Title.

PS3556.034M9   1985   813'.54   85-16304
ISBN 0-89865-419-X (lim. ed.)
ISBN 0-89865-414-9 (pbk.)

Printed in the United States of America

myth ADVENTURES one

Introduction

Welcome to the dubious worlds of **Myth Adventures.**

For those of you who are enjoying your first exposure to these wacky escapades, as well as for those loyal readers who have been following the exploits from their first appearance, Donning/Starblaze has asked that I provide a brief glimpse as to how the volume in your hand came to pass.

I began writing professionally in 1976 with an action adventure science fiction novel titled **Cold Cash War.** It was a grim little piece, full of friends double-crossing each other and wounded mercenaries burying themselves while they are still alive. . . one belly laugh after another, right? As the work progressed, I noticed something about the effect it was having on me. Specifically, if I wrote that stuff more than three nights in a row, I started looking at people funny on the streets. . . and at work, and at home. . . you get the picture. To save my own sanity, I decided I needed another writing project to work on to use as a break from the mood **Cold Cash** was generating. Obviously, this new project should be as different from **Cold Cash** as I could make it.

With that goal in mind, I began to scratch-build a new project. In some ways, it was very easy. All I had to do was take the mirror image of what I was already writing. **CCW** was grim, so the new project should be funny. Similarly, since **CCW** was science fiction, why not make the new work fantasy? This "reverse approach" continued into the project itself. Most heroic fantasy centers around a sword-swinging main character, usually pitted against the dark powers of a sorcerer or five. This time, why not look at things from the sorcerer's point of view? Since it was supposed to be humorous, make it a pretty inept sorcerer. . . an apprentice, maybe. That brings up the question of a teacher. . . .

Progressing in this manner, the first *Myth* book, **Another Fine Myth,** began to take shape. I will freely and publicly acknowledge that one of the greatest influences on the formation of the characters was a festival of Bob Hope/Bing Crosby *Road* movies that was airing on late-night TV while I

was working on the concept. That was the overall mood of "anything goes" fun that I wanted in my book. Front and center in those movies are two characters who can talk their way into or out of any kind of trouble, although mostly they talk their way into it. . . and Aahz and Skeeve came into being.

It was a fun project and served its purpose of providing distraction so I could finish my "serious work." Then Donning/Starblaze bought it (that's right, the same ones who are publishing this new illustrated color version) and the rest is history. Reader demand convinced us that the book should become a series, and **Another Fine Myth** was followed by **Myth Conceptions, Myth Directions, Hit or Myth, Myth-Ing Persons,** and, most recently, **Little Myth Marker.**

Somewhere along the way, I started talking to Richard Pini from WaRP Graphics about an illustrated adaptation. The key requirement would be the proper artist. . . or improper, as the case may be. I have been friends with Phil Foglio for over a decade now, and an admirer of his comic genius for the same period of time. Foglio was the illustrator-cover artist for the Donning/Starblaze *Myth Adventure* novels and it was apparent that he had a unique feel for the characters. Once before, we had double-teamed a project (*The Capture*) which was nominated for a Hugo in 1976. We had a lot of fun working on that project. I imagined we could have a lot of fun working on **Myth Adventures** also. Like me, Phil has never been the kind of guy to say "No" to fun. For **Myth Adventures,** all that was really necessary was to feed him the material and stand back.

The first compilation of that project is what you are currently holding. It is my sincere hope that you find in it what I did when I first created the characters. . . diversion. When things get a little too grim in your life, enjoy a few laughs on Aahz and Skeeve. It will help keep things in perspective.

Oh. . . and have fun, too.

Robert Asprin
Ann Arbor, Michigan
August, 1985

1

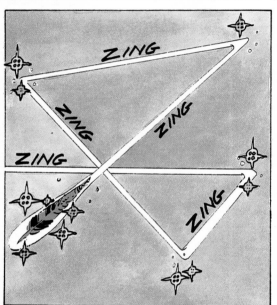

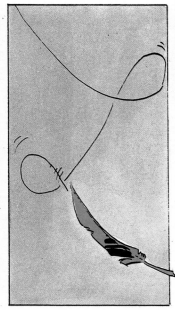

GOOD ENOUGH, LAD. NOW *PUT IT BACK IN THE BOOK.*

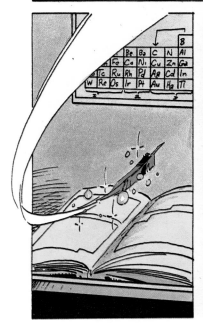

CHOMP!

HUMPH! A TRIFLE SHOWY —

BUT EFFECTIVE.

3

4

BUT— IT WENT OUT.

NEVER YOU MIND THAT. YOU LIT IT!

YOU HAVE THE CONFIDENCE NOW— NEXT TIME IT'LL BE *EASY!* BY THE STARS, WE'LL MAKE A MAGICIAN OUT OF YOU YET!

NOW EAT!

I'LL ADMIT I *WAS* BEGINNING TO DISPAIR, LAD. WHAT MADE THAT LESSON SO HARD? HAS IT OCCURED TO YOU THAT YOU COULD USE THAT SPELL TO GIVE YOU EXTRA LIGHT WHEN PICKING A LOCK? OR EVEN TO START A FIRE TO SERVE AS A DIVERSION?

I THOUGHT ABOUT IT. BUT EXTRA LIGHT MIGHT DRAW UNWANTED ATTENTION. AND A FIRE, WELL, THAT COULD HURT SOMEONE...

...AND I DON'T WANT TO HURT:

WHOOPS.

SMAK!

I THOUGHT SO!! YOU'RE *STILL* PLANNING TO BE A *THIEF* — TO USE *MY* MAGIC TO *STEAL!*

WHAT OF IT?! IT BEATS *STARVING.* WHAT'S SO GOOD ABOUT BEING A MAGICIAN, ANYWAY?

IT WAS GOOD ENOUGH FOR YOU WHEN THE WINTER DROVE YOU OUT OF THE WOODS TO STEAL — "BEATS SLEEPING UNDER A BUSH," YOU SAID.

IT *STILL* DOES — THAT'S WHY I'M HERE. BUT HIDING IN A HUT IN THE MIDDLE OF THE WOODS ISN'T MY IDEA OF A FUTURE. YOU WERE LIVING ON ROOTS AND BERRIES UNTIL *I* CAME ALONG AND STARTED TRAPPING MEAT FOR THE FIRE.

MAYBE THAT'S YOUR IDEA OF A WONDERFUL LIFE.... BUT IT'S NOT *MINE!!*

5

PERHAPS YOU'RE RIGHT, SKEEVE.

PERHAPS I'VE BEEN SHOWING YOU ALL THE WORK OF MAGIC, BUT NONE OF THE REWARDS.

I FORGET HOW SUPPRESSED MAGIC IS IN THESE LANDS.

YOU SHOULD KNOW THAT NOT ALL LANDS ARE LIKE THIS ONE.

NOR WAS *I* ALWAYS AS YOU SEE ME NOW.

IN PLACES WHERE MAGIC IS RECOGNIZED INSTEAD OF FEARED, IT IS RESPECTED AND COMMISSIONED BY THOSE IN POWER.

THERE A SKILLFUL MAGICIAN WHO KEEPS HIS WITS ABOUT HIM CAN REAP A *HUNDRED* TIMES THE WEALTH YOU ASPIRE TO AS A MERE THIEF.

AND POWER...

SUCH *POWER* THAT...

AH, YES — BUT YOU AREN'T IMPRESSED BY WORDS, ARE YOU, LAD? COME. I'LL GIVE YOU A DEMONSTRATION OF THE POWER YOU MAY SOMEDAY WIELD.

IF YOU PRACTICE YOUR LESSONS, THAT IS.

6

EVEN DEMONSTRATIONS SHOULD PROVIDE A LESSON. CONTROL, SKEEVE.

CONTROL IS THE MAINSTAY OF MAGIC.

POWER WITHOUT CONTROL INVITES DISASTER.

THAT IS WHY YOU PRACTICE WITH A FEATHER, THOUGH YOU ARE ABLE TO MOVE MUCH LARGER AND HEAVIER OBJECTS.

CONTROL.

EVEN *YOUR* MEAGER POWERS WOULD BE DANGEROUS UNLESS CONTROLLED.

...AND I WILL NOT TEACH YOU MORE UNTIL YOU'VE *LEARNED* THAT CONTROL.

TO DEMONSTRATE I WILL NOW SUMMON FORTH A **DEMON.**

HE IS POWERFUL, CRUEL, VICIOUS AND WOULD KILL US BOTH IF GIVEN THE CHANCE. YET DESPITE THIS WE NEED NOT FEAR HIM...

BECAUSE HE WILL BE CONTROLLED.

HE WILL BE UNABLE TO HARM US AS LONG AS HE IS CONTAINED *WITHIN* THAT PENTAGRAM. BUT IF WE SHOULD LOSE THAT PROTECTION...

WHAT DO YOU MEAN *IF?!*

NOW WATCH, SKEEVE—YOU'LL LEARN MUCH IF WE SURVIVE.

WHAT DO YOU MEAN IF?!

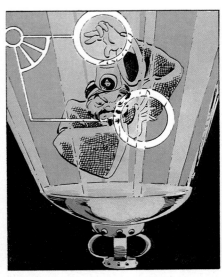

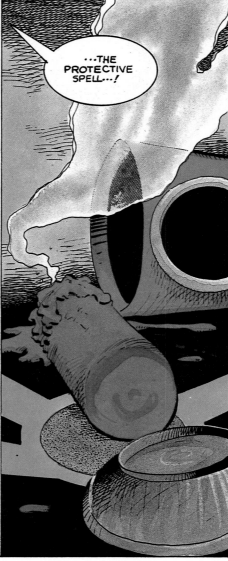

12

UM— YOU ARE A DEMON, AREN'T YOU?

HUH? OH, YEAH, I GUESS YOU COULD SAY I AM.

WELL...IF YOU DON'T MIND MY ASKING — WHY DON'T YOU ACT LIKE ONE?

❊SIGH❊ EVERYBODY'S A CRITIC.

KID, WOULD YOU BE HAPPIER IF I TORE YOUR THROAT OUT?

UM, WELL... IF YOU PUT IT THAT WAY...

FOR THAT MATTER, WHO ARE YOU ANYWAY? YOU COME WITH THE ASSASSIN?

NO!

WITH HIM, GARKIN! I'M... I WAS HIS STUDENT!

NO KIDDIN'— GARKIN'S APPRENTICE?

PLEASED TO — WHAT'S WRONG?

UH—WELL, YOU ARE A DEMON...

YEAH, SO?

WELL, DEMONS ARE SUPPOSED TO BE···

BE WHAT?

UM···· COLD, VICIOUS AND BLOODTHIRSTY?

13

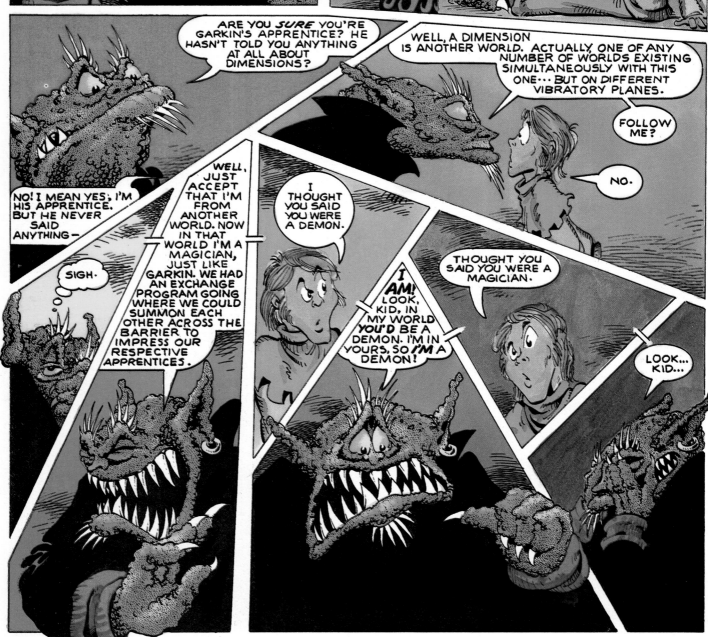

14

LET ME TRY IT THIS WAY...

ARE YOU GONNA SHAKE MY HAND OR AM I GONNA RIP YOUR HEART OUT?!

HII'MSKEEVEPLEASEDTOMEETYOU!

PLEASED TO MEETCHA, KID. I'M AAHZ.

OZ?

NO RELATION.

RELATION TO WHAT?

NEVER MIND. HUMPH. THERE'S CERTAINLY NOTHING HERE TO AROUSE THE GREEDY SIDE OF HIS FELLOW BEINGS. EARLY PRIMITIVE – ENDURING DECOR, BUT HARDLY SOUGHT AFTER.

CRAK!

WE LIKE IT.

DON'T GET YOUR BACK UP, KID. I'M JUST LOOKING FOR A MOTIVE.

MOTIVE?

A REASON FOR SOMEONE TO OFF OLD GARKIN. I'M NOT BIG ON VENGEANCE, BUT HE **WAS** A DRINKING BUDDY OF MINE AND IT'S GOT MY CURIOSITY UP.

HOW ABOUT YOU, KID? CAN YOU THINK OF ANYTHING? YOU'VE GOT A VESTED INTEREST IN THIS TOO, YOU KNOW— **YOU** MIGHT BE THE NEXT TARGET.

ME?! BUT THE GUY WHO DID IT IS DEAD.

DOESN'T THAT FINISH IT?

WAKE UP, KID. SEE? GOLD CLOAK. THIS WAS A PROFESSIONAL ASSASSIN. SOMEBODY **HIRED HIM,** AND COULD HIRE ANOTHER ONE.

HELLO... WHAT'S THIS?

CLUNK THUMP

SEEMS LIKE **I'M** NOT THE ONLY DEMON ABOUT.

A DEVIL!

A WHAT? OH, A DEEVIL. NO, IT'S NOT FROM DEVA. IT'S FROM **IMPER.** AN IMP. DIDN'T GARKIN TEACH YOU ANYTHING?

WHAT?

HEY— WAIT A MINUTE. WHAT'S THIS?

IT LOOKS LIKE A CROSSBOW.

WITH HEAT SEEKING, ARMOR-PIERCING QUARRELS? IS THAT GOVERNMENT ISSUE IN THIS WORLD?

HEAT SEEKING...

NEVER MIND, KID, I DIDN'T THINK SO.

THIS DEFINITELY DOES NOT LOOK GOOD.

TAP TAP

NOW THE QUESTION IS (CRUNCH) WHO WOULD BE *CRASS* ENOUGH ... (CRUNCH CRUNCH CRUNCH)

...TO HIRE AN IMP (MUNCH) FOR AN 'ASSASSIN'. (GULP CRUNCH)

THE ONLY ONE I CAN (SLURRRP! AH!) THINK OF IS ISSTVAN (GULP) BUT THAT'S IMPOSSIBLE.

ARF GAG RETCH

OH — YOU'VE HEARD OF HIM?

WHY—

YES! THAT WAS THE NAME THE ASSASSIN GAVE!

ISSTVAN! THIS CHANGES EVERYTHING. IF HE'S UP TO HIS OLD TRICKS THEN THERE ISN'T A MOMENT TO LOSE.

WAIT A MINUTE — WHAT'S GOING ON?

HEY! YOU SAID I MIGHT BE A *TARGET!*

COULDN'T YOU HELP ME?

COULDN'T I COME WITH YOU?

TAKE TOO LONG TO EXPLAIN, KID. SEE YOU.

YEAH — WELL, THAT'S THE WAY IT CRUMBLES. TELL YOU WHAT — START RUNNING.

NO TIME. I'VE GOTTA MOVE.

YOU'D JUST GET IN THE WAY — AND MIGHT EVEN GET ME KILLED.

BUT WITHOUT YOU *I'LL* BE KILLED!

TELL YOU WHAT, KID, I'VE REALLY GOT TO GET GOING — BUT JUST TO SHOW YOU I THINK YOU'LL SURVIVE, I'LL SHOW YOU A LITTLE TRICK YOU MIGHT USE SOMETIME. YOU SEE ALL THIS CRUD GARKIN USED TO BRING ME ACROSS THE BARRIER? WELL, IT'S NOT NECESARY.

WATCH CLOSE AND I'LL SHOW YOU HOW WE DO IT WHEN THE APPRENTICES AREN'T AROUND.

CRACK-RAK-AK!   SNAP!! POP-KRAK!

17

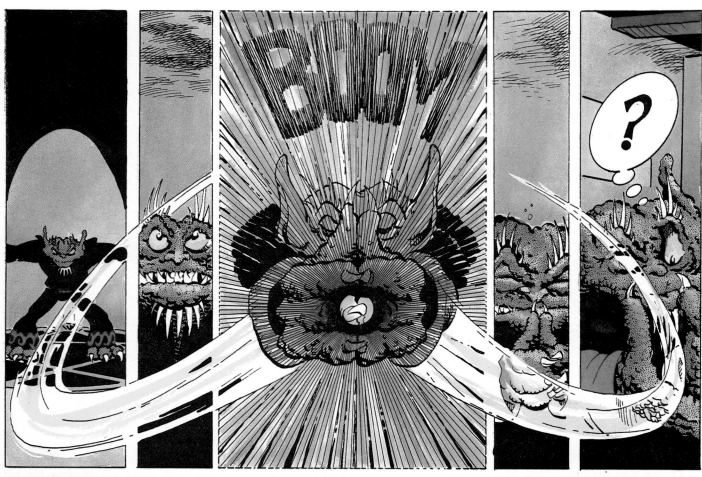

18

ISLIACIVIS ARZIŪMIH... ZŪ ZXEHIHII ON ÔV/ŽI.3 N ĠV.H GSII!!

OH NO.

THAT'S GOT TO BE IT! GARKIN, YOU ILLCONCEIVED SON OF A WOMBAT—

WHAT'S A WOMBAT?

WOMBAT

NEVER MIND—I DON'T WANT TO KNOW.

AAHZ— WHAT'S THE MATTER?

GARKIN DID THIS TO ME— GARKIN, THAT NO GOOD GOATFISH! GARKIN, YOUR LOUSY...

—TEACHER.

SKEEVE... GOLLY, I GUESS I HAVEN'T BEEN CLEAR ABOUT THINGS.

UM, THAT'S OKAY—I WAS JUST WONDERING...

YOU SEE, SKEEVE, THE SITUATION IS THIS. GARKIN AND I HAVE BEEN PLAYING JOKES ON EACH OTHER FOR SOME TIME NOW. IT STARTED ONCE WHEN WE WERE DRINKING AND HE STIFFED ME WITH THE BILL...

WELL, THE NEXT TIME I SUMMONED HIM I BROUGHT HIM IN OVER A LAKE - AND HE HAD TO DO HIS DEMON ACT ARMPIT DEEP IN WATER.

HE GOT EVEN BY...

...WELL, I WON'T BORE YOU WITH DETAILS. BUT WE'VE GOTTEN INTO THE HABIT OF PUTTING EACHOTHER INTO THESE EMBARASSING SITUATIONS.

BUT THIS TIME- THIS TIME THE OLD FROG KISSER'S GONE TOO FAR.

DON'T YOU AGREE?

YOU STILL HAVEN'T TOLD ME WHAT'S WRONG.

WHAT'S WRONG IS THAT STINKING SLIME MONGER TOOK AWAY MY POWERS!

I CAN'T DO A FLAMING THING UNLESS HE REMOVES HIS STUPID, PRANKISH SPELL AND HE CAN'T 'CAUSE HE'S DEAD!

COMPRENDO, FLYBAIT?

WELL, IF THERE WAS ANYTHING I COULD DO...

THERE IS, SKEEVE. MY BOY - ALL YOU HAVE TO DO IS FIRE UP THE OLD CAULDREN OR WHATEVER AND REMOVE THIS SPELL!

I CAN'T DO THAT.

WHAT DO YOU WANT? BLOOD? IF YOU'RE TRYING TO HOLD ME UP, I'LL...

I CAN'T DO IT BECAUSE I CAN'T DO IT. I DON'T KNOW HOW!

HUMM. THAT COULD BE A PROBLEM. WELL, JUST POP ME BACK INTO MY OWN DIMENSION AND I'LL GET SOMEONE THERE TO TAKE IT OFF.

I CAN'T DO THAT EITHER. REMEMBER I TOLD YOU I'VE NEVER EVEN HEARD OF DIMENSIONS!

21

WELL, KID – IT LOOKS LIKE WE'RE STUCK WITH EACH OTHER. THE SET UP ISN'T IDEAL BUT IT'S TIME TO BITE THE BULLET AND PLAY THE CARDS WE'RE DEALT.

YOU *DO* KNOW WHAT CARDS *ARE*, DON'T YOU?

OF COURSE.

GOOD.

WHAT'S A BULLET?

URG!

KID – THERE'S A GOOD CHANCE THAT THIS PARTNERSHIP IS GONNA DRIVE ONE OF US CRAZY. UNLESS YOU KNOCK OFF THE DUM-DUM QUESTIONS EVERY OTHER SENTENCE, IT'S GONNA BE *ME*!

BUT I CAN'T UNDERSTAND HALF OF WHAT YOU'RE SAYING!

TELL YA WHAT. TRY TO SAVE UP THE QUESTIONS AND ASK THEM *ALL* AT ONE TIME, ONCE A DAY. OKAY?

I'LL TRY.

GREAT! NOW HERE'S THE SITUATION AS I SEE IT. IF ISSTVAN IS HIRING IMPS FOR ASSASSINS ...

WHAT'S AN IMP?

GULP GULP GULP

BETTER. NOW, WHAT WAS I TALKING ABOUT?

RIGHT.

GLAK❊

– IMPS.

IF ISSTVAN'S HIRING IMPS AND ARMING THEM WITH NON-SPEC WEAPONS IT CAN ONLY MEAN HE'S UP TO HIS OLD TRICKS. NOW, SINCE I DON'T HAVE *MY* POWERS, I CAN'T GET OUT OF HERE TO SOUND THE ALARM. THAT'S WHERE *YOU* COME IN, KID ...

WE'LL...

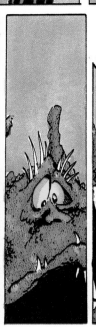

WHAT THE HELL'S THE MATTER WITH *YOU* ?!!

I'M SORRY, AAHZ–

I DON'T UNDERSTAND A SINGLE THING YOU'VE SAID.

SUCKER

SIGH.

HEY, KID, DON'T BEAT ON YOURSELF. IT'S NOT YOUR FAULT IF GARKIN WAS TIGHT WITH HIS SECRETS.

NOBODY EXPECTS YOU TO KNOW SOMETHING YOU WEREN'T TAUGHT.

I JUST FEEL SO STUPID.

I'M NOT USED TO FEELING STUPID.

YOU AREN'T STUPID, KID—GARKIN WOULDN'T HAVE TAKEN YOU FOR AN APPRENTICE IF YOU WERE.

IF ANYBODY HERE'S STUPID — IT'S ME. I GOT SO CARRIED AWAY THAT I TRIED TALKING TO AN APPRENTICE AS IF HE WERE A FULL BLOWN MAGICIAN. NOW THAT'S STUPID.

HEY, KID— RIGHT NOW YOU CAN DO MORE MAGIC THAN I CAN.

BUT YOU KNOW MORE.

BUT I CAN'T USE IT!

EXIT

SNIFF

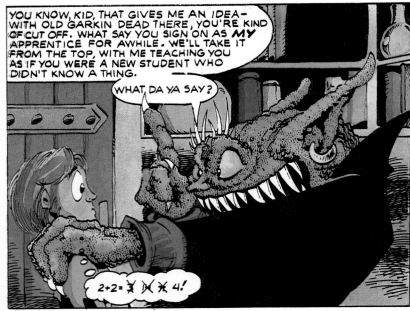

YOU KNOW, KID, THAT GIVES ME AN IDEA— WITH OLD GARKIN DEAD THERE, YOU'RE KIND OF CUT OFF. WHAT SAY YOU SIGN ON AS **MY** APPRENTICE FOR AWHILE. WE'LL TAKE IT FROM THE TOP, WITH ME TEACHING YOU AS IF YOU WERE A NEW STUDENT WHO DIDN'T KNOW A THING.

WHAT DA YA SAY?

2+2= ~~3~~ ~~X~~ ~~X~~ 4!

GEE—THAT SOUNDS **GREAT**, AAHZ!

YES IT DOES, DOESN'T IT?

THEN IT'S A DEAL?

IT'S A **DEAL!**

WHAT'S THAT?

BUT...

BUT YOU SAID...

MY WORD ISN'T **GOOD** ENOUGH FOR YOU?

THAT'S RIGHT—YOU'RE MY APPRENTICE NOW: FIRST LESSON:

I DON'T GO AROUND SHAKING HANDS WITH **APPRENTICES!!**

GOT THAT?

GOOD. HERE'S YOUR SECOND LESSON.

YES, MASTER AAHZ.

IN A CRISIS YOU DON'T WASTE ENERGY WISHING FOR INFO AND SKILLS YOU AIN'T GOT. NOW SHUT UP WHILE I FILL YOU IN ON THE SITUATION... APPRENTICE.

24

NOW YOU KNOW A LITTLE ABOUT DIMENSIONS AND THAT MAGICIANS CAN OPEN PASSAGES BETWEEN THEM. WELL, VARIOUS MAGICIANS USE THAT POWER FOR VARIOUS REASONS. GARKIN USED TO OPEN THE BARRIERS JUST FOR LAUGHS. OTHERS DO IT FOR PROFIT...

Y'SEE, *DIFFERENT DIMENSIONS HAVE DIFFERENT* TECHNOLOGIES **SOME** MAGICIANS - SMUGGLERS REALLY - USE THIS TO THEIR OWN ADVANTAGE. THEY BUY AND SELL TECHNOLOGIES ACROSS BARRIERS TO GAIN POWER MOST OF THE INVENTORS IN ANY DIMENSION ARE, IN FACT, CLOSET MAGICIANS.

NOW, ACTUALLY THEY'RE A FAIRLY ETHICAL BUNCH, BUT ONCE IN A WHILE YOU GET A BAD ONE WHO WON'T ADHERE TO THE SMUGGLER'S CODE - YOU *DON'T* PROVIDE ADVANCED TECHNOLOGY TO A BACKWARD DIMENSION.

WHICH BRINGS US TO ISSTVAN...

SOME SAY ISSTVAN ISN'T PLAYING WITH A FULL DECK - I THINK HE'S BEEN PLAYING WITH HIS WAND TOO MUCH - BUT WHATEVER - HE WANTS TO RULE THE DIMENSIONS. ALL OF THEM. HE'S TRIED IT BEFORE, BUT WE GOT WIND OF IT IN TIME AND A BUNCH OF US TEAMED UP AND STOPPED HIM. THAT WAS WHEN I FIRST MET GARKIN. I THOUGHT ISSTVAN HAD GIVEN UP AFTER HIS LAST DRUBBING. AND NOW THIS.

"POWER. EACH DIMENSION HAS A CERTAIN AMOUNT OF MAGIC POWER WHICH IS SHARED BY THAT WORLD'S MAGICIANS. IF ISSTVAN CAN ELIMINATE ALL THE OTHER MAGICIANS HE CAN USE ALL THE MAGICAL ENERGY TO ATTACK *ANOTHER* DIMENSION. IF HE WINS *THERE* HE HAS THE ENERGY OF *TWO* DIMENSIONS TO DRAW ON TO ATTACK A THIRD AND SO ON. THE LONGER HE GOES, THE STRONGER HE'LL GET— AND THE HARDER HE'LL BE TO STOP"

BUT *WHY* DOES HE WANT TO TAKE OVER EVERYTHING?

WHY... I *UNDERSTOOD* THAT.

GOOD. THEN YOU UNDERSTAND *WHY* WE'VE GOT TO STOP HIM.

WE? YOU MEAN US? YOU AND ME?!

I KNOW. IT'S NOT MUCH BUT IT'S ALL WE GOT.

AAHZ—TELL ME THE TRUTH—DO YOU THINK YOU CAN TEACH ME ENOUGH TO HAVE A CHANCE OF STOPPING HIM?

OF *COURSE*, KID. I WOULDN'T EVEN *TRY* IF WE DIDN'T HAVE A CHANCE.

WHY—WE'LL BE *FAMOUS* FOR THIS! LIKE NAPOLEON AT WATERLOO—CUSTER AT THE LITTLE BIG HORN—THE LIGHT BRIGADE AT BALACLAVA...

GEE, AAHZ—YOU REALLY THINK SO?

KID—WHY WOULD *I* LIE TO YOU?

26

DON'T GIVE ME ANY LIP, BOY! I'M DOING MY DAMNDEST TO KEEP US FROM GETTING KILLED!!!

I'M SORRY, AAHZ. IF I KNEW WHAT YOU WERE DOING, I COULD HELP.

WHAT'S A...

I'M MAINLY LOOKING FOR WEAPONS. YOU KNOW—SWORDS, KNIVES, BAZOOKAS...

SKIP IT.

WEAPONS? I THOUGHT YOU WERE A MAGICIAN.

OH NO—I'M NOT GOING THROUGH THAT AGAIN. BESIDES, WHAT'S THAT GOT TO DO WITH WEAPONS? I'VE LOST MY POWERS... REMEMBER?

WELL, IT'S JUST THAT I'VE NEVER KNOWN A MAGICIAN WHO USED WEAPONS.

AND HOW MANY MAGICIANS HAVE YOU KNOWN?

UH... ONE.

AND LOOK WHAT HAPPENED TO HIM.

I'LL HELP YOU LOOK.

I'M ALREADY FINISHED. WE'VE GOT A SWORD WITH A CRUDDY BLADE, BAD BALANCE AND FAKE JEWELS IN THE HANDLE—AND TWO KNIVES THAT HAVEN'T BEEN SHARPENED SINCE THEY WERE MADE.

I ALSO FOUND SOME GOLD STUFF WE CAN CONVERT INTO CASH.

COLESKI

28

BUT THOSE THINGS ARE CURSED!

NAW — THAT'S JUST A STORY MAGICIANS TELL TO KEEP THIEVES AWAY.

THEN NONE OF THESE THINGS HAVE ANY MAGIC POWERS?

NOW I DIDN'T SAY *THAT*. OCCASIONALLY YOU STUMBLE ACROSS A REAL *ITEM* —

BUT THEY'RE PRETTY RARE.

SO HOW CAN YOU TELL THE REAL FROM THE FAKE?

SO GARKIN DIDN'T EVEN TEACH YOU TO SEE AURAS. TIME FOR ANOTHER LESSON, APPRENTICE.

HAVE YOU EVER DAYDREAMED? YOU KNOW, JUST STARED AT SOMETHING AND LET YOUR MIND DRIFT···

OKAY, NOW LOWER YOUR HEAD TO TABLE LEVEL AND LOOK ACROSS THE TABLE AT THE WALL. DON'T FOCUS ON ANYTHING — JUST STARE AND LET YOUR MIND DRIFT.

UM··· YES.

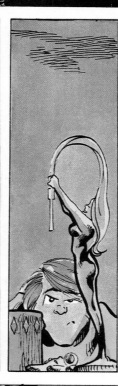
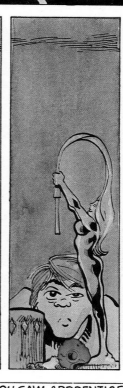

HEY?!

WHAT WAS IT, KID?

WELL, JUST FOR A SECOND THERE, I THOUGHT I SAW A RED GLOW AROUND THE *RING*.

THE RING, EH? THAT FIGURES. THEN THE REST OF THIS STUFF SHOULD BE OKAY.

NOW WHAT YOU SAW, APPRENTICE, WAS AN *AURA*. MOST PEOPLE HAVE THEM, SOME PLACES DO AND IT'S A SURE TEST TO CHECK IF AN ITEM'S TRULY MAGICAL. I'D BET THIS RING IS WHAT GARKIN USED TO FRY THE ASSASSIN.

ARE WE GOING TO TAKE IT WITH US?

DO *YOU* KNOW HOW TO CONTROL IT?

WELL... NO.

NEITHER DO I. THE LAST THING WE NEED TO CART AROUND IS A RING THAT SHOOTS FIRE. *PARTICULARLY* IF WE DON'T KNOW WHAT ACTIVATES IT.

SO WE LEAVE IT. IF WE'RE LUCKY, THE OTHERS WILL FIND IT AND FRY THEMSELVES.

WHAT OTHERS?

HMMM? OH – THE OTHER ASSASSINS.

WHAT OTHER ASSASSINS?!

KID, ASSASSINS *NEVER* WORK ALONE. THAT'S WHY THEY NEVER MISS. THERE'S A BACK-UP TEAM AROUND HERE SOMEWHERE.

YOU MEAN WHILE WE'VE BEEN FOOLING AROUND WITH SWORDS AND AURAS THERE'VE BEEN MORE ASSASSINS ON THE WAY?!

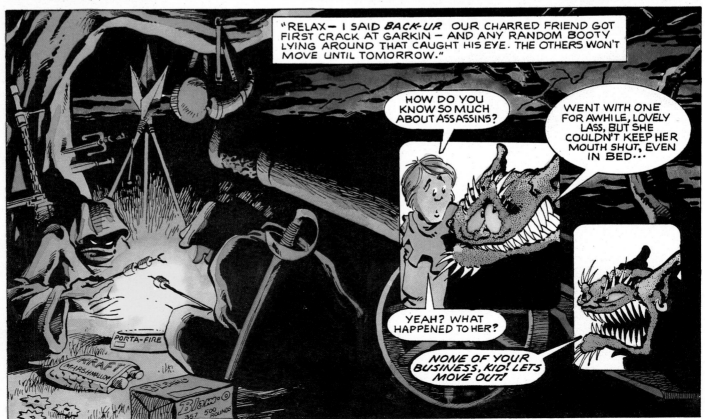

"RELAX – I SAID *BACK-UP.* OUR CHARRED FRIEND GOT FIRST CRACK AT GARKIN – AND ANY RANDOM BOOTY LYING AROUND THAT CAUGHT HIS EYE. THE OTHERS WON'T MOVE UNTIL TOMORROW."

HOW DO YOU KNOW SO MUCH ABOUT ASSASSINS?

WENT WITH ONE FOR AWHILE, LOVELY LASS, BUT SHE COULDN'T KEEP HER MOUTH SHUT, EVEN IN BED···

YEAH? WHAT HAPPENED TO HER?

NONE OF YOUR BUSINESS, KID! LETS MOVE OUT!

PORTA-FIRE

KRAFT MARSHMALLOW

357 500 ROUNDS

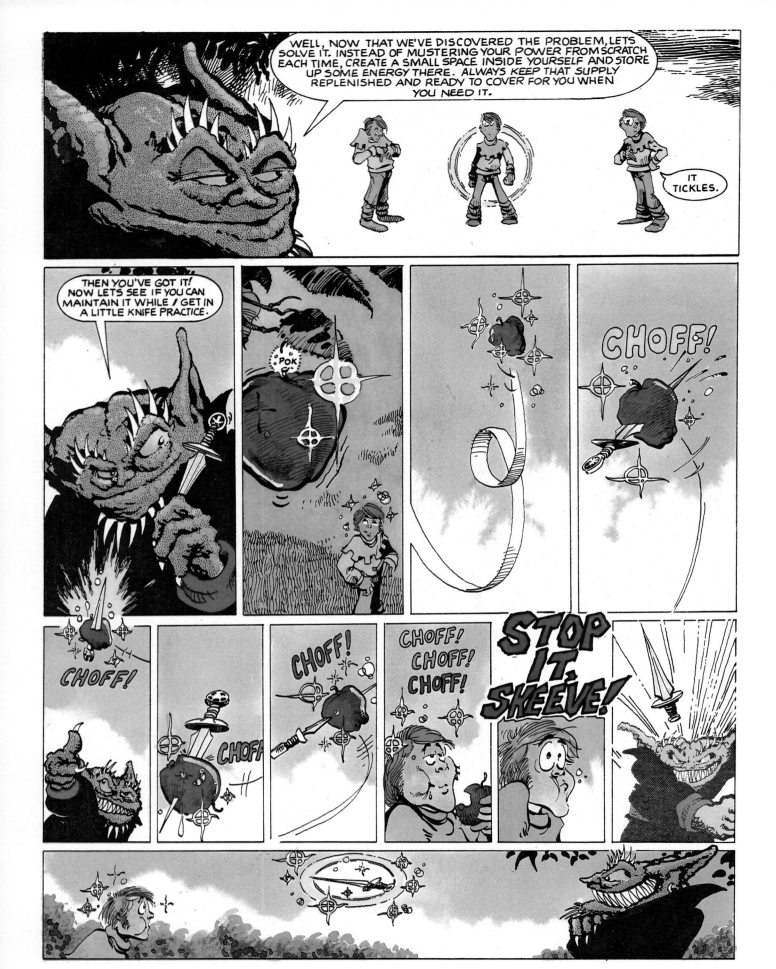

I DID IT!

NOW *THAT'S* THE STUFF TO HAVE CONFIDENCE IN.

THAT LITTLE PIECE OF MAGIC WILL SAVE YOUR LIFE SOMEDAY.

VORP!

AND IN THE NICK OF TIME TOO; SOMEONE'S COMING.

HOW CAN YOU TELL?

NOTHING SPECIAL. I'VE JUST GOT BETTER HEARING THAN YOU. DON'T PANIC, IT ISN'T THE IMPS.

ONE ANIMAL, WITH A RIDER.

WELL, AREN'T WE GOING TO *HIDE*?

NOT THIS TIME— I'M GOING TO TEACH YOU A NEW SPELL, RIGHT NOW, WHILE YOU'RE HOT! WE'VE GOT A FEW MINUTES.

MINUTES? I CAN'T LEARN A SPELL IN A FEW *MINUTES!*

SURE YOU CAN. THIS ONE'S EASY. ALL YOU'VE GOT TO DO IS *DISGUISE* ME TO LOOK HUMAN.

HOW DO I DO THAT?

THE SAME WAY YOU DO EVERYTHING ELSE; WITH YOUR MIND. FIRST CLOSE YOUR EYES. OKAY, NOW PICTURE ANOTHER FACE.

"UM···WHO?"

"ANYBODY."

"GOT ONE."

GARKIN

"GOOD. NOW PICTURE ME."

"YEAH?"

"NOW BLANK OUT MY FEATURES···"

"···AND MOLD THE FACE TO THE HUMAN FEATURES."

"THIS ISN'T EASY."

"GOT IT?"

"UM··· I DUNNO···"

"WELL, JUST KEEP THAT IMAGE IN THE BACK OF YOUR MIND."

NOW OPEN YOUR EYES!

IT DIDN'T WORK!

SURE IT DID.

BUT... BUT YOU HAVEN'T CHANGED... SORT OF.

TRUST ME. *YOU* CAN'T SEE IT BECAUSE *YOU* CAST THE SPELL, AND SO YOUR MIND ISN'T FOOLED BY THE ILLUSION. EVERYONE *ELSE* WILL BE. GARKIN HUH? WELL, IT'LL DO FOR NOW.

YOU REALLY SEE GARKIN'S FACE?

SURE, WANT TO LOOK?

AAHZ... I CAN'T *SEE* YOU.

WELL, KID, I'VE NEVER BEEN ONE TO ENGAGE IN UNDUE REFLECTION...

I HEAR SOMEBODY!

GET IT?

ARE YOU *SURE* ABOUT THIS, AAHZ?

TRUST ME, KID — THERE'S NOTHING TO WORRY ABOUT.

"RELAX, SKEEVE", "THIS'LL BE EASY, SKEEVE", "TRUST ME, SKEEVE"... BOY, WHEN YOU MISS A CALL, YOU DON'T DO IT SMALL, DO YOU?

SHUT UP, KID.

I DON'T WANT TO SHUT UP! I WANT TO KNOW WHAT HAPPENED TO THAT 'EASY SPELL' YOU TAUGHT ME!

I WAS WONDERING ABOUT THAT MYSELF. HMMM. CHECK HIS AURA AND LOOK FOR ANYTHING UNUSUAL.

"TRUST ME", YOU SAID, "I KNOW..."

HEY!

WHAT IS IT?

"HIS AURA! IT'S SORT OF REDDISH YELLOW EXCEPT THERE'S A BLUE PATCH ON HIS CHEST."

I THOUGHT SO... HA! LOOK AT THIS!

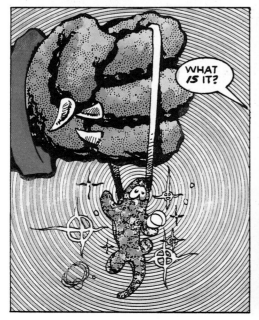

WHAT IS IT?

I'M NOT SURE... BUT I'VE GOT A HUNCH. I WANT YOU TO REMOVE THE DISGUISE SPELL.

BUT... OH, ALL RIGHT.

39

WELL?

PERFECT. ♥

TERRIFIC. NOW WHAT?

NOW PAY ATTENTION.

OY

DID ANYBODY GET THE NUMBER OF THAT···

RELAX, STRANGER, THINGS ARE NOT AS THEY SEEM.

BEWARE DEMON! I AM NOT WITHOUT DEFENSES!

OH? SUCH AS?

SUCH AS MY SWORD···

UH OH···

THEN FACE MY DAGGER···

ER···

THROWING AXE?···

SHURIKENS?···

SKINNING KNIFE?···

BRASS KNUCKLES?···

HMMM. I MIGHT JUST HAVE TO RIP YOU APART WITH MY BARE HANDS. MESSY BUT EFFECTIVE.

RELAX— I'M NOT A DEMON.

HA! KNOW YOU, DEMON, THAT THIS CHARM ENABLES ME TO LOOK THROUGH ANY SPELL AND SEE YOU AS YOU REALLY ARE!

40

41

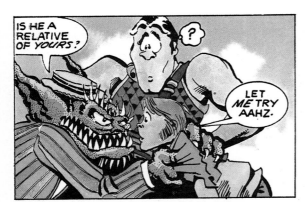

IS HE A RELATIVE OF YOURS?

?

LET ME TRY AAHZ.

LOOK, WHAT HE'S TRYING TO SAY IS THAT IF HE WERE A DEMON, HE WOULDN'T LOOK LIKE A DEMON, BECAUSE IF HE WAS HE WOULDN'T, BUT HE DOSEN'T, SO HE ISN'T, SO HE CAN'T.

OH, I GET IT!

WELL, NOW YOU'VE LOST ME!

BUT IF YOU AREN'T A DEMON, WHY DO YOU LOOK LIKE ONE?

ACCURSED!

SIMPLE, I AM... ACCURSED!

YES, AN OCCUPATIONAL HAZARD...

FOR I AM... AAHZ! DEMON HUNTER EXTRORDINAIRE!

NEVER HEARD OF YOU.

"HOW FLEETING FAME. TRUST ME. ANYWAY, I ACHIEVED GREAT RENOWN AMONG THE DEMONS DUE TO MY UNPRECEDENTED SUCCESS. INDEED, WHEN IT WAS LEARNED I WAS COMING, MOST DEMONS WOULD EITHER FLEE THE TERRITORY OR KILL THEMSELVES."

OH WOE! IT IS AAHZ!

WE MUST FLEE...

OR KILL OURSELVES!

DOES HE ALWAYS BRAG THIS MUCH?

HE'S JUST GETTING STARTED.

42

YES, BEFORE HE EXPIRED, THE DEMON HAD WORKED A *SPELL* UPON ME CAUSING ME TO APPEAR AS A *DEMON* TO ALL WHO BEHOLD ME.

FIENDISH. CLEVER, BUT FIENDISH.

WISH I COULD DO SOMETHING TO HELP.

WHY... MAYBE YOU *CAN* QUIGLEY, OLD PAL.

I DON'T SEE HOW. I'M JUST A DEMON HUNTER.

PRECISELY WHAT WE ARE IN NEED OF. YOU SEE, WE'RE BEING *FOLLOWED* BY DEMONS.

HMMM, I DUNNO, I'M ALREADY *ON A MISSION,* AND I HATE TO BOOK MYSELF UP IN ADVANCE.

OH YOU WOULDN'T HAVE TO GO OUT OF YOUR WAY. JUST WAIT RIGHT HERE, AND THEY'LL BE ALONG PRESENTLY.

WELL, **THAT'S** CONVENIENT. WHY ARE THEY AFTER YOU?

"A VILE MAGICIAN SENT THEM AFTER I WAS FOOLISH ENOUGH TO SEEK HIS AID ··· THE CURSE, YOU KNOW. LITTLE DID I KNOW *HE* WAS IN LEAGUE WITH DEMONS."

OF COURSE. WAIT A MINUTE··· WAS THAT MAGICIAN NAMED *GARKIN,* BY ANY CHANCE?

WHY, AS A MATTER OF FACT IT *WAS.* DO YOU KNOW HIM?

DO TELL.

HE'S MY MISSION! THE MAN I'M OFF TO KILL.

FOR HAVING TRAFFIC WITH DEMONS, YOU KNOW, THE USUAL.

"WHY *EVERYONE* HAS HEARD OF THE TERRIBLE *GARKIN,* BOY, BUT ALL THOUGHT HIM VANISHED LONG AGO. THEN THREE WEEKS BACK, I LEARNED FROM AN INNKEEPER NAMED ISSTVAN — A SINCERE ENOUGH FELLOW — IF A BIT STRANGE — THAT HE'D *REAPPEARED* AND WAS UP TO HIS OLD TRICKS."

HOW DID YOU HEAR OF *GARKIN?*

"BUT WE WERE TALKING ABOUT *YOUR* PROBLEM, SIRS. HOW MANY DEMONS DID YOU SAY THERE WERE?"

"JUST TWO, QUIG, WE'VE CAUGHT GLIMPSES OF THEM OCCASIONALLY."

WELL...I SUPPOSE THAT SINCE IT *WAS* GARKIN THAT SENT THEM OUT... VERY WELL, I'LL DO IT! I'LL ASSIST YOU IN YOUR *BATTLE.*

THAT'S GREAT. EXCEPT WE WON'T *BE* THERE.

WHY NOT? I SHOULD THINK THAT YOU'D *WELCOME* THE CHANCE ONCE THE ODDS WERE EVEN.

IF *I* WERE HERE THERE WOULD BE NO FIGHT... MY REPUTATION AND ALL. IF THEY SAW ME HERE THEY WOULD SIMPLY *FLEE.*

FRANKLY, I FIND THAT *HARD* TO BELIEVE.

WELL, I MUST ADMIT THAT MY *CHARMED SWORD DOES* HAVE SOMETHING TO DO WITH IT.

CHARMED SWORD?

HMMM? OH, YES, IT WAS WILLED TO ME BY THE FAMOUS DEMON HUNTER ALFONZ DI CARLO, KILLER OF OVER 200 DEMONS.

IT IS SAID THAT WHOEVER WIELDS IT CANNOT BE KILLED BY A DEMON.

"REALLY? NEVER HEARD OF HIM. HOW DID HE DIE?"

"KNIFED BY AN EXOTIC DANCER. TERRIBLE."

"YES, THEY'RE NASTY THAT WAY. BUT ABOUT THE SWORD — DOES THE CHARM WORK?"

WELL, I HAVEN'T BEEN KILLED BY A DEMON SINCE I USED IT.

AND DEMONS ACTUALLY *RECOGNIZE* IT AND FLEE, EH?

EXACTLY.

OF COURSE I HAVEN'T HAD OCCASION TO USE IT FOR YEARS. BEEN TOO BUSY TRYING TO GET THIS CURSE REMOVED. SOMETIMES I'VE THOUGHT OF SELLING IT, BUT IF I EVER GET BACK INTO THE BIZ, IT'LL BE A BIG HELP IN RE-ESTABLISHING MY *REPUTATION.*

HMM. TELL YOU WHAT, JUST TO GIVE A HAND TO A FELLOW DEMON HUNTER DOWN ON HIS *LUCK,* I'LL TAKE IT OFF YOUR HANDS FOR 5 GOLD PIECES.

FIVE?! YOU MUST BE JOKING! I COULDN'T LET IT GO FOR LESS THAN 200!

AH WELL, THAT COUNTS ME OUT. ALL I'VE GOT IS 50.

K-CHING!

46

BUT... BUT...

YES, I MUST BE OFF. THANK YOU FOR YOUR ASSISTANCE, MY FRIENDS. SAFE JOURNEY.

GOOD LUCK.

HEY! COME BACK HERE!

NOW WHAT WAS THE BIG RUSH TO GET RID OF HIM? AS GULLIBLE AS HE WAS, I COULD'VE TRADED HIM OUT OF HIS PANTS!

BASICALLY, I WANTED HIM ON HIS WAY BEFORE HE CAUGHT ON TO THE FLAW IN YOUR STORY.

FLAW?! LET'S HEAR THIS BIG FLAW.

LOOK, HE SAW THROUGH MY DISGUISE-MAGIC BECAUSE OF THE PENDANT THAT LETS HIM SEE THROUGH SPELLS, RIGHT?

RIGHT. AND I EXPLAINED IT AWAY BY SAYING I WAS THE VICTIM OF A DEMON'S CURSE.

WHICH CHANGED YOUR APPEARANCE WITH A SPELL- BUT IF HE COULD SEE THROUGH SPELLS, HE SHOULD BE ABLE TO PENETRATE THAT ONE TO SEE YOU AS A NORMAL MAN.

RIGHT?

MAYBE WE'D BETTER BE ON OUR WAY NOW THAT WE KNOW WHERE ISSTVAN IS.

HONEST AAHZ

TELL ME, AAHZ, WHAT WOULD YOU DO IF YOU ENCOUNTERED A DEMON HUNTER AS SMART AS ME?

THAT'S EASY. I'D KILL HIM.

THINK ABOUT IT.

THREE DAYS LATER.

OKAY, KID, THAT'S ENOUGH FOR TODAY. EAT YOUR LIZARD-BIRD AND GET SOME SLEEP.

DO YOU WANT ME TO REMOVE YOUR DISGUISE?

NAH. TONIGHT WE'LL SEE IF YOU CAN HOLD IT IN YOUR SLEEP.

AAHZ? HOW WOULD YOU SAY MY POWERS STACK UP AGAINST THE DEVILS?

THE ASSASSINS FOLLOWING US.

WHAT DEVILS?

I TOLD YOU—THOSE ARE IMPS AND EVEN IF THEY GOT PAST QUIGLEY THEY'RE NOT GOING TO CATCH US.

WELL ANYWAY, WHAT'S THE DIFFERENCE BETWEEN THEM?

DEEVILS ARE SOME OF THE MEANEST CHARACTERS AROUND — THE MOST FEARED AND RESPECTED CHARACTERS IN THE DIMENSIONS.

WHAT ARE THEY? WARRIORS? SORCERERS?

WORSE.

THEY'RE MERCHANTS.

MERCHANTS?!

DON'T SNEER, KID, MAYBE MERCHANT IS TOO SEDATE A WORD. TRADERS SUPREME IS MORE LIKE IT.

"AT ONE TIME THE ENTIRE DIMENSION OF DEVA BECAME BLIGHTED AND COULDN'T SUPPORT ANY LIFE AT ALL. PLANT, ANIMAL, INSECT, FISH, NOTHING. DIMENSION TRAVEL, ONCE A FRIVOLOUS PASTIME, NOW BECAME THE KEY TO SURVIVAL. MANY LEFT DEVA AND MIGRATED TO OTHER DIMENSIONS. THEIR TALES OF A BARREN, MISERABLE HOMELAND SERVED AS A PROTOTYPE FOR MANY RELIGIOUS GROUPS' CONCEPT OF AN AFTERWORLD FOR EVIL SOULS."

"THE ONES WHO *STAYED*, HOWEVER, DECIDED TO USE THE POWER OF DIMENSION TRAVEL IN A DIFFERENT WAY. THEY ESTABLISHED THEMSELVES AS TRADERS, TRAVELING THE DIMENSIONS, BUYING AND SELLING WONDERS. WHAT IS COMMON IN ONE DIMENSION IS FREQUENTLY RARE IN ANOTHER. AS THE PRACTICE GREW, THESE TRADERS BECAME RICH AND POWERFUL, NOT TO MENTION THE SHREWDEST HAGGLERS ANYWHERE. THEY'RE SCATTERED THROUGHOUT THE DIMENSIONS, RETURNING TO DEVA ONLY OCCASIONALLY TO VISIT — *THE BAZAAR*."

NO ONE CAN TRAVEL TO ALL THE DIMENSIONS IN ONE LIFETIME. THE BAZAAR ON DEVA IS THE PLACE THE DEEVILS MEET TO TRADE WITH EACH OTHER, AND ANY OTHER TRAVELER WHO DARES TO DEAL WITH THEM. IT'S SAID THAT IF YOU MAKE A DEAL WITH A DEEVIL, YOU'D BE WISE TO COUNT YOUR FINGERS AFTERWARD, THEN YOUR ARMS AND LEGS, THEN YOUR RELATIVES···

IMPS. *PFAWG!* THEY'RE CHEAP IMITATIONS!

I GET THE IDEA. NOW WHAT ABOUT IMPS?

"THEIR DIMENSION, IMPER, LIES CLOSE TO DEVA. THE DEEVILS BARGAIN WITH THEM SO OFTEN THAT THE IMPS ARE ALMOST BANKRUPT FROM ALL OF THE IRRESISTABLE '*FAIR DEALS*' THEY ARE OFFERED."

49

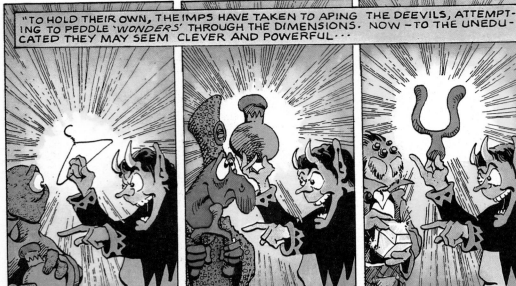

AAHZ? HOW DID QUIGLEY KNOW ABOUT GARKIN? HE MADE GARKIN SOUND LIKE A... A LEGEND INSTEAD OF AN INCOMPETENT.

INCOMPETENT? WHAT MAKES YOU SAY THAT?

I WAS WITH GARKIN FOR OVER A YEAR AND BARELY LEARNED TO LIGHT A CANDLE. I'VE BEEN WITH YOU LESS THAN TWO WEEKS AND I'M DOING ALL KINDS OF STUFF.

YEAH, IT DOES KINDA MAKE GARKIN LOOK BAD, DON'T IT.

KID, GARKIN USED TO BE THIS DIMENSION'S *WIZARD-IN-RESIDENCE*, IF YOU WILL. HE WASN'T ONE OF THE GREATS. BUT HE WAS KNOWN AND RESPECTED THROUGHOUT THE MANY WORLDS.

WHAT HAPPENED?

"REMEMBER I TOLD YOU THAT A BUNCH OF US TOOK CARE OF ISSTVAN THE LAST TIME HE ACTED UP?"

"WELL, AT THAT FINAL BATTLE, GARKIN WAS WITH US."

BUT··· HE··· DIDN'T MAKE IT.

WHAT DO YOU MEAN? GARKIN DIDN'T DIE···

DID HE?

KID··· SOMEDAY YOU'LL LEARN THAT A MAGICIAN CAN DO THINGS TO YOU THAT ARE INFINITELY WORSE THAN DYING.

...OH.

WHY DIDN'T HE TELL ME ANY OF THIS? I WAS HIS APPRENTICE!

GOOD QUESTION. WHY DIDN'T HE? CAN YOU THINK OF ANY REASON WHY HE WOULDN'T'VE TRUSTED YOU?

YOU WANT TO USE MY MAGIC TO STEAL!!

NO··· I CAN'T THINK OF ANYTHING.

I DIDN'T THINK SO. GARKIN WOULDN'T HAVE TAKEN YOU ON UNLESS HE THOUGHT YOU WERE SOMETHING SPECIAL.

AAHZ? WHAT DIMENSION DO YOU COME FROM?

...DOES THAT MAKE YOU A PERVERT?

PERV.

NO, THAT MAKES ME A PER*VECT!*

NOW SHUT *UP!*

AAHZ?

WHAT DIMENSION IS THIS?

NOW WHAT?

ER...

SIGH.

THIS IS KLAH, KID.

...WHAT DOES THAT MAKE *ME,* AAHZ?

AAHZ?

SHHHHHHH!

AAHZ, WHAT IS IT?

I THINK WE GOT COMPANY, KID.

53

UH... ER... I...

YES, THROCKWODDLE, AND AREN'T YOU GOING TO INTRODUCE ME TO YOUR COLLEAGUES?

UH... ER... I...

PERHAPS HE DOESN'T REMEMBER US.

NONSENSE! HIS TWO OLDEST FRIENDS BROCKHURST AND HIGGINS? HOW COULD HE POSSIBLY FORGET OUR NAMES? JUST BECAUSE HE FORGOT TO SHARE THE LOOT DOESN'T MEAN HE'D FORGET OUR NAMES -- BE FAIR, HIGGINS.

FRANKLY, BROCKHURST- I'D RATHER HE REMEMBERED THE LOOT AND FORGOTTEN OUR NAMES.

UH... ER... I...

GENTLEMEN -- LET ME SAY WHAT A GREAT PLEASURE IT IS...

AS THIS IS A PRIVATE MATTER BETWEEN THE THREE OF US, I'D ADVISE YOU TO STAY OUT OF IT, WHOEVER YOU ARE.

UH... ER... I...

BROCKHURST- IT OCCURS TO ME WE MAY BE BEING A BIT HASTY IN OUR ACTIONS.

TRUE, HIGGINS, THERE MIGHT BE A PERFECTLY SIMPLE EXPLANATION FOR ALL THIS.

THANK YOU, GENTLEMEN.

IT IS ALSO POSSIBLE THAT PIGS CAN FLY.

NOW THAT WE'VE GOT THESE TWO, WE SHOULD ALSO SECURE OUR TRAVELING COMPANION BEFORE WE CONTINUE THIS DISCUSSION.

THINK!

I SUPPOSE YOU'RE RIGHT. WHY DON'T *YOU* FETCH HIM ALONG WHILE I STAND WATCH HERE?

SSSTHUP!

MY DEAR *BROCKHURST*, I *REFUSE* TO APPROACH THAT BEAST ALONE.

CHOK!

AND *WHAT* IS TO KEEP THESE TWO FROM BEATING A HASTY RETREAT?

TOK! TOK! TOK!

NICE GROUPING.

—THE FACT THAT WE'LL BE WATCHING THEM FROM SOMEWHERE IN THE DARKNESS WITH CROSSBOWS SHOULD GIVE THEM PAUSE, I THINK.

CRUNCH!

TRUE, AND *THROCKWODDLE*, I SUGGEST YOU NOT ATTEMPT TO AVOID US FURTHER. WHILE I DON'T *BELIEVE* WE COULD BE ANY MORE UPSET WITH YOU THAN WE ARE RIGHT NOW, THAT WOULD CERTAINLY BE THE WAY TO FIND OUT.

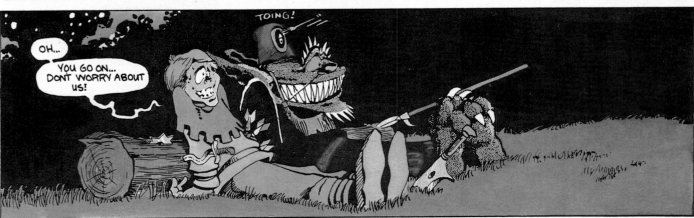

TOING!

OH... YOU GO ON... DON'T WORRY ABOUT US!

55

THIS SHOULD BE AMUSING...

- BY THE GODS BELOW...

...A PERVERT!

I'LL ONLY SAY THIS ONCE ... THAT'S PERVECT!

YESSIR!!

NOW THAT THAT'S SETTLED WHY DON'T YOU PUT AWAY THOSE SILLY CROSSBOWS AND SIT DOWN SO WE CAN CHAT LIKE CIVILIZED FOLK, EH?

YESSIR!

YESSIR! BUT... WHY ARE YOU HERE, SIR — IF YOU DON'T MIND MY ASKING...

"SIMPLE ENOUGH. I WAS SUMMONED ACROSS THE DIMENSIONS BY ONE GARKIN, A MAGICIAN I HAVE NEVER CARED MUCH FOR.."

" IT SEEMS HE WAS EXPECTING TROUBLE FROM A RIVAL AND WAS EAGER TO ENLIST MY AID."

I REFUSED.

GARKIN AND I WERE ABOUT TO COME TO BLOWS IN A SORCEROUS BATTLE OF TRULY EARTH-SHAKING PROPORTIONS..."

"...WHEN WHO SHOULD APPEAR BUT *THROCKWODDLE!*"

"WHOSE SPECTACULAR ENTRANCE SO PUT GARKIN OFF HIS GUARD..."

GLUNK TUNG!

"...THAT *THROCKWODDLE* WAS ABLE TO DO ME THE FAVOR OF PUTTING A QUARREL INTO THE OL' SLIME-STIRRER WITH IMPUNITY."

"NATURALLY WE FELL TO CHATTING AFTER-WARDS."

YOU ANSWERED QUESTIONS ABOUT AN ASSIGNMENT?!

WOULDN'T *YOU*, CONSIDERING THE CIRCUM-STANCES?

OH, YES, OF COURSE.

ANYWAY, IT OCCURED TO ME THAT I OWED THIS *ISSTVAN* FELLOW A FAVOR.

SO I HAD *THROCKWODDLE* HERE TAKE ME TO HIM.

YOU COULD HAVE WAITED FOR US.

" HE MENTIONED THAT HIS ACTION AGAINST *GARKIN* HAD BEEN PART OF AN ASSIGNMENT FOR ONE '*ISSTVAN.*' "

WELL... I WANTED TO... BUT... UM...

...BUT I INSISTED. MY TIME IS QUITE VALUABLE AND I'M NOT ABOUT TO WASTE IT WAITING AROUND.

YOU COULD'VE LEFT US A MESSAGE.

WE *DID!* I RECORDED A MESSAGE ONTO MY RING, AND I *KNOW* YOU FOUND IT AS I SEE IT ON YOUR HAND!

WHAT?! *THIS?* BUT THIS ISN'T A MESSAGE RING.

WHAT DO YOU MEAN?! I JUST BOUGHT IT!

NOSSIR! HONEST-- IT'S A FIRE RING. YOU PRESS AGAINST IT WITH THE FINGERS ON EITHER SIDE.

DEW TELL.

SEE?

VADABLAM!!

AAiiee!!

TERRIBLY SORRY ABOUT THAT, *HIGGINS.*

WELL I'D APPRECIATE ITS RETURN. THERE'S A CERTAIN DEVEEL MERCHANT I'LL HAVE TO TEST IT UPON WHEN I RETURN.

YESSIR!

CAN WE WATCH?

NOW THAT WE'VE GOTTEN THAT SETTLED, WHO OR WHAT IS *THAT?*

WE AREN'T AT ALL SURE OURSELVES.

IT'S ALL QUITE PUZZLING, REALLY.

"IT HAPPENED ABOUT THREE DAYS BACK. WE WERE FOLLOWING YOUR TRAIL ... "

THANKS, GUYS.

OH DEAR. TERRIBLY SORRY, THROCKWODDLE.

WELL NOW THAT YOU'VE *REMEMBERED*, *TELL* ME ABOUT THIS DEVEEL.

ASK *BROCKHURST*. HE SEEMS TO BE EAGER TO TALK ABOUT IT.

WELL, THERE ISN'T MUCH ELSE. THERE'S A DEVEEL, *FRUMPLE* IN RESIDENCE IN TWIXT. HE GOES UNDER THE COVER OF *ABDUL* THE RUG MERCHANT, BUT HE DOES A BRISK BUSINESS TRADING ACROSS THE DIMENSIONS.

SO WHAT'S HE DOING IN KLAH? THERE CAN'T BE MUCH BUSINESS HERE.

WELL, RUMOR HAS IT THAT HE WAS EXILED FROM DEVA AND IS HIDING HERE, ASHAMED TO SHOW HIMSELF IN A MAJOR DIMENSION.

EXILED ?!! WHAT DID HE *DO*?

THEY SAY HE ACTUALLY GAVE SOMEONE A REFUND!

I'M SURPRISED THEY DIDN'T KILL HIM!!

HMMM. DOES *ISSTVAN* KNOW OF *FRUMPLE'S* EXISTENCE?

I DON'T THINK SO, ELSE HE'D EITHER HAVE ENLISTED HIM OR HAD HIM ASSASSINATED.

GOOD! THEN HE COULD VERY WELL BE THE KEY TO OUR PLOT!

PLOT? WHAT PLOT?

OUR PLOT AGAINST *ISSTVAN*, OF COURSE!

PPPPFFF!!

HACK·AK·AK COUGH! SPUTTER GASP!

WHAT?!! ARE YOU INSANE?

NO, BUT *ISSTVAN* IS — I MEAN, THINK: HAS HE BEEN ACTING PARTICULARLY STABLE?

NO, BUT THEN I NEVER MET A MAGICIAN WHO *DID*! PRESENT COMPANY INCLUDED! BESIDES, I THOUGHT YOU WERE ON YOUR WAY TO HELP HIM?

THAT WAS BEFORE I HEARD YOUR STORY. I'M NOT EAGER TO ASSOCIATE WITH A MAGICIAN WHO PITS HIS EMPLOYEES AGAINST EACH OTHER.

WHEN DID HE DO THAT?

REMEMBER THE DEMON HUNTER OVER THERE? HE ALL BUT SAID THAT *ISSTVAN* SENT HIM.

YEAH, SO?

SO?! *ISSTVAN* SENT HIM TO *KILL* YOU! EITHER HE WAS TRYING TO CUT HIS OVERHEAD BY ASSASSINATING HIS ASSASSINS, OR HE'S SO MENTALLY UNSTABLE THAT HE'S LASHING OUT BLINDLY AT EVERYONE.

EITHER WAY IT DOESN'T SOUND TOO GOOD.

YOU KNOW... I THINK HE'S GOT A POINT.

BUT... IF THIS IS TRUE ... THEN WHAT ARE WE TO DO?

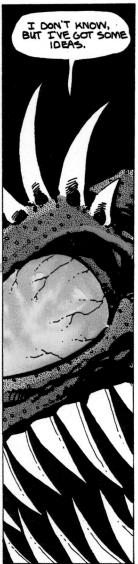

I DON'T KNOW, BUT I'VE GOT SOME IDEAS.

YOU GO BACK TO *ISSTVAN*. DON'T SAY ANYTHING OR HE MIGHT CONSIDER YOU DANGEROUS. STAY NEAR HIM. LEARN AS MUCH ABOUT HIM AS POSSIBLE, BUT DON'T DO ANYTHING UNTIL WE GET THERE.

WHERE ARE *YOU* GOING?

WE'RE GOING TO HAVE A CHAT WITH *FRUMPLE*. AGAINST *ISSTVAN* THE SUPPORT OF A DEVEEL WOULD BE INVALUABLE.

WHAT DO YOU MEAN "WE"? ISN'T *THROCKWODDLE* COMING WITH US?

!

NO, I'VE DEVELOPED A... FONDESS FOR HIS COMPANY. TELL *ISSTVAN* THAT *GARKIN* KILLED HIM.

BESIDES, IF *FRUMPLE* REFUSES TO HELP US, A GOOD ASSASSIN WILL BE HANDY.

PERVERT

A ○—————○← B

WELL, WHAT ABOUT THE DEMON HUNTER?

C R U M P

I'LL TELL YOU WHAT WE DO WITH HIM...

WE'LL TAKE HIM WITH US!

OKAY, I'M READY.

GOOD! TODAY WE'RE GOING TO TEACH YOU TO *FLY!!*

FLY?

YEP, *FLY!!* EXCITING, ISN'T IT?

WHY?

WHADYA MEAN, *WHY?* EVER SINCE WE FIRST CAST JEALOUS EYES ON THE BIRDS OF THE AIR, WE'VE LONGED TO FLY. NOW YOU'RE GETTING A CHANCE. *THAT'S* WHY IT'S EXCITING. *EVERYBODY* WANTS TO FLY!

I DON'T...

WHY *NOT?*

I'M AFRAID OF HEIGHTS.

THAT'S NO REASON NOT TO LEARN.

OKAY KID, LET ME PUT IT THIS WAY: YOU'RE MY APPRENTICE...

I HAVEN'T HEARD A GOOD REASON YET AS TO WHY I SHOULD.

AND I'M NOT GOING TO HAVE AN APPRENTICE WHO CAN'T *FLY!!*

GOT ME?

GOT'CHA, *AAHZ.*

HOW DOES IT WORK?

ACTUALLY IT DOESN'T INVOLVE ANYTHING YOU DON'T KNOW ALREADY.
YOU KNOW HOW TO LEVITATE OBJECTS, RIGHT? WELL ALL FLYING IS IS LEVITATING YOURSELF. INSTEAD OF STANDING ON THE GROUND AND LIFTING AN OBJECT — YOU PUSH AGAINST THE GROUND AND LIFT YOURSELF!

THAT'S *IT?*

THAT'S IT. NOW FIND A FORCE LINE, HOOK INTO IT, AND GIVE IT A TRY.

70

71

BARKEEP!! TWO FLAGONS OF WINE!!

SO WHEN DO WE GO?

WILL YOU RELAX? A FEW MINUTES WON'T HURT. BESIDES — LOOK...

CUSTOMERS, SEE? WE CAN'T DO ANYTHING UNTIL THEY LEAVE. SO HAVE A DRINK AND RELAX.

WHAT'S TAKING THEM SO LONG?

MAYBE THEY CAN'T MAKE UP THEIR MINDS.

C'MON, KID, THE SHOP'S NOT THAT BIG.

WE'VE WAITED LONG ENOUGH, LET'S GO.

BUT THAT COUPLE IS STILL INSIDE.

WELL WE'LL JUST HAVE TO... INSPIRE THEM TO CONCLUDE THEIR BUSINESS WITH MORE SPEED, EH?

?!

MAY I HELP YOU GENTLEMEN?

SPECIAL HOOKE RU

AH... WE'D LIKE TO TALK TO *ABDUL*?

I AM HE AND HE IS I. YOU SEE BEFORE YOU *ABDUL*, A MERE SHADOW OF A MAN, PUSHED TO THE BRINK OF STARVATION BY HIS CLEVER CUSTOMERS! I LOSE MONEY ON EVERY SALE, BUT A MAN MUST EAT!

ACTUALLY, WE'RE LOOKING FOR SOMETHING IN A DEEP SHAG POLYESTER WALL-TO-WALL CARPET.

POLY...?! WHERE'D YOU LEARN YOUR MANNERS? I GOTTA *LIVE* IN THIS TOWN!

SORRY, *FRUMPLE*.

I'LL BET. FOLKS AROUND HERE ARE REAL INTOLERANT OF STRANGE HAPPENINGS, SO WATCH IT. IF THEY KNEW I WAS A DIMENSION-HOPPER, THEY'D ROAST ME!

OUT TO LUNCH

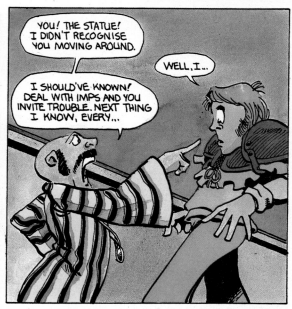

YOU! THE STATUE! I DIDN'T RECOGNISE YOU MOVING AROUND.

I SHOULD'VE KNOWN! DEAL WITH IMPS AND YOU INVITE TROUBLE. NEXT THING I KNOW, EVERY...

WELL, I...

SAY...

WAITAMINUTE...

I MIGHT'VE KNOWN. WOULD YOU DROP THE *DIS-GUISES?* I LIKE TO KNOW WHO I'M DEALING WITH.

OY! A PERVERT!! THIS I DON'T NEED!

THAT'S PER*VECT* IF YOU WANT TO DO BUSINESS WITH US.

THAT'S PER*VERT* UNTIL I SEE YOUR MONEY!

73

74

TRUCE?

FOR SOME REASON PERVERTS AND DEVEELS HAVE NEVER GOTTEN ALONG.

THAT'S PERVECT!

SEE WHAT I MEAN?

AAHZ, JUST TELL HIM!!

LOOK, FRUMPLE HERE'S THE THING; I'VE LOST MY POWERS.

WHAT?!! YOU CAME HERE WITHOUT EVEN THE MAGICAL ABILITY TO PROTECT YOURSELF AGAINST BEING FOLLOWED ?!!

LOOK, THE SOONER YOU CURE MY PROBLEM, THE SOONER WE'LL LEAVE.

OH ALL RIGHT! PROBABLY THE ONLY WAY I'LL GET RID OF YOU.

HMMM

HMMM?

HM-MMM

WELL?

HMMM? OH- WELL YOUR POWERS ARE GONE ALL RIGHT.

SO HOW DID YOU LOSE THEM?

NO KIDDING.

I DON'T KNOW FOR SURE. I WAS SUMMONED TO KLAH BY A MAGICIAN, AND WHEN I GOT HERE, THEY WERE GONE.

A MAGICIAN? WHO?

GARKIN.

GARKIN?! YOU WANT TO IN-VOLVE ME IN A FIGHT WITH GARKIN?!

GET OUT!

IT'S ONLY ON GARKIN'S SUFFERANCE THAT I CAN STAY HERE! I SAID, GET...

GARKIN'S DEAD!

THERE ARE SOME THINGS YOU DON'T JOKE ABOUT, PERVERT.

GARKIN'S DEAD, FRUMPLE, AND YOU'RE THE FIRST PERSON BESIDES THE KID AND ME TO KNOW IT, WHO ISN'T DEAD AS WELL.

DID YOU...?

NO, SKIP IT... I DON'T WANT TO KNOW. NOW ABOUT THESE LOST POWERS OF YOURS; YES, I CAN HELP, BUT IT'LL COST YOU.

HOW MUCH DO YOU HAVE WITH YOU?

WELL, WE HAVE MRRRF...

SUPPOSE YOU TELL US WHAT YOU CONSIDER A FAIR PRICE.

HMMM, WELL... MATERIALS COST IS UP, AND OF COURSE THERE'S MY TIME... AND YOU DID CALL WITHOUT AN APPOINTMENT... LET'S SAY, JUST AS A ROUGH ESTIMATE MIND YOU, IN THE NEIGHBORHOOD OF... SAY!

MAYBE YOU'D BE WILLING TO WORK THIS OUT IN TRADE! I CURE YOU, YOU DO ME A LITTLE FAVOR.

WHAT KIND OF FAVOR?

OH... A SMALL THING... SORT OF A DECOY MISSION.

WE'D RATHER PAY CASH.

SHUT UP, KID — WHAT ARE THE DETAILS?

YOU MIGHT'VE NOTICED THE YOUNG COUPLE THAT ENTERED MY SHOP BEFORE YOU. YES? GOOD.

YOU'VE ALSO NOTICED THEIR ABSENCE THEN. I'LL GET TO THAT IN A MOMENT. AS TO THEIR STORY... I'LL SPARE YOU THE DETAILS BUT TO SAY THAT THEY'RE YOUNG LOVERS KEF APART BY THEIR FAMILIES.

"IN THEIR DESPERATION THEY TURNED TO ME FOR ASSISTANCE."

"I OBLIGED THEM BY SENDING THEM TO ANOTHER DIMENSION WHERE THEY CAN BE FREE OF THEIR FAMILIES' INTERFERENCE."

FOR A FEE OF COURSE.

WELL OF *COURSE* FOR A FEE! WHADDYA THINK I AM?

C'MON *AAHZ*, IT SOUNDS LIKE A DECENT THING TO DO, EVEN IF IT WAS FOR A FEE.

YOU GOT IT KID! WHAT A SWEET-HEART HE IS! LAST CHANCE TO GET IN ON THE RUG BUSINESS, KID?

NO? AH.

ANYWAY, MY GENEROSITY MIGHT'VE GONE BEYOND THE BOUNDS OF GOOD SENSE. I MEAN, EVEN *YOU* NOTICED THEM COMING IN BUT NOT OUT.

IF THEIR RELATIVES SUCCEED IN TRACKING THEM HERE AND NO FURTHER...

MUST'VE BEEN *SOME* FEE.

NOW HERE'S THE DEAL; IN EXCHANGE FOR MY ASSISTANCE, YOU TWO DISGUISE YOURSELVES AND LAY A FALSE TRAIL OUT OF MY SHOP. NOTHING ELABORATE, JUST LET YOURSELVES BE SEEN LEAVING TOWN. BY THE TIME YOU GET BACK, I'LL HAVE YOUR CURE ALL READY.

DEAL?

YOU WOULDN'T HAPPEN TO HAVE A SKIRT FOR THE KID, WOULD YOU?

OH NO YOU DON'T!! THERE IS NO WAY THAT...

78

WELL... COULDN'T WE TRAVEL BY LESS CROWDED STREETS?

C'MON, KID, NOBODY'S GONNA KNOW YOU WHEN YOU'RE DISGUISED...

...BESIDES, YOU DON'T EVEN *KNOW* ANYBODY IN THIS TOWN.

DOCK'S

I JUST DON'T LIKE IT, THAT'S ALL.

TOO BAD. BEING SEEN IS PART OF OUR DEAL WITH *FRUMPLE*. IF YOU HAD ANY OBJECTIONS YOU SHOULD'VE RAISED THEM BEFORE WE CLOSED THE DEAL.

I DIDN'T KNOW **THIS** WAS INCLUDED IN THE DEAL!!!

ANY OTHER PROBLEMS?

WELL, YEAH,... WHAT ARE WE DOING?

WHAT'VE YOU GOT? AMNESIA? WE'RE LAYING A FALSE TRAIL FOR...

NO, NO, I KNOW *THAT.* I MEAN WHY ARE WE DOING *FRUMPLE* A FAVOR INSTEAD OF JUST PAYING HIS PRICE?

YOU WOULDN'T ASK IF YOU'D EVER DEALT WITH A *DEVEEL* BEFORE. THEIR PRICES ARE SKY-HIGH, ESPECIALLY IF THEY KNOW THEIR CUSTOMERS ARE DESPERATE — LIKE US.

JUST BE THANKFUL WE GOT SUCH A GOOD DEAL.

THAT'S WHAT I MEAN. ARE YOU SURE THIS IS SUCH A GOOD DEAL?

WHAT *DO* YOU MEAN?

WELL, FROM WHAT *I'VE* BEEN TOLD...

...IF YOU THINK YOU'VE GOTTEN A GOOD DEAL FROM A *DEVEEL*...

...IT USUALLY MEANS YOU'VE OVER-LOOKED SOMETHING.

AND NATURALLY YOU SPEAK FROM A WIDE RANGE OF EXPERIENCE...

WHO TOLD YOU SO MUCH ABOUT DEALING WITH *DEVEELS?*

YOU DID.

UM.

A-HMMM. YOU'RE RIGHT, KID. I MIGHT'VE BEEN A BIT HASTY.

SO WHAT DO WE DO?

WELL, NORMALLY I DEAL HONESTLY...

WHAT?!!

SHADDAP.

BUT SINCE THERE'S A GOOD CHANCE WE'RE BEING DOUBLE-CROSSED, START LOOK-ING FOR A PRIVATE PLACE WHERE WE CAN DROP THESE DISGUISES.

KNIVES

SALE

OKAY, I GOT A FEW POSSIBILITIES SPOTTED.

WELL, FORGET IT. START LOOKING FOR SOME-PLACE WIDE OPEN, WITH A LOT OF EXITS.

WHY THE CHANGE IN STRATEGY?

TAKE A LOOK OVER YOUR SHOULDER, *CASUAL*-LIKE.

AAHZ... WE'RE BEING FOLLOWED!!

HEY KID, I TOLD *YOU*, REMEMBER?

BUT WHY? WHAT DO THEY WANT?

I DON'T KNOW...

...BUT I'M WILLING TO BET IT HAS SOMETHING TO DO WITH THESE *DISGUISES*.

THEN WHY DON'T I JUST CHANGE US BA—*ACK!!*

BAF!

BAD IDEA!

I'D RATHER HAVE THEM MAD AT WHO THEY *THINK* WE ARE THAN HAVE 'EM FIND OUT WE'RE MAGICIANS.

SO WHAT *DO* WE DO?

WE KEEP WALKING ~CALMLY~ UNTIL WE FIND SOMEONE IN AUTHORITY WHO'LL GIVE US PROTECTION.

WE'LL BE OKAY AS LONG AS WE DON'T SHOW 'EM WE'RE SCARED.

BONK!

—OR WE CAN STOP *RIGHT* NOW AND FIND OUT WHAT THIS IS ALL *ABOUT* !!!!

85

WELL, WHAT DID YOU EXPECT? IF YOU'D WANTED OUR HELP, YOU SHOULDN'T HAVE INCLUDED US ON YOUR LIST OF CUSTOMERS.

IF IT HAD BEEN UP TO US, WE'D HAVE STRUNG YOU UP A WEEK AGO! BUT THESE YOKELS GAVE YOU MORE TIME.

AH WELL... ANYBODY GOT A ROPE?

PSST, KID!

MORE ADVICE?

YEAH— WHEN THEY HANG YOU — FLY! YOU KNOW, LIKE I TAUGHT YOU!

THEY'D SHOOT ME DOWN!

NOT FLY AWAY, JUST HOVER AT THE END OF THE ROPE AND TWITCH. THEY'LL THINK YOU'RE HANGING.

BUT AAHZ! I CAN'T LEVITATE BOTH OUR BODIES... I'M NOT THAT GOOD YET!

YOU'RE WOBBLING, PRIVATE.

...AND KEEP UP MY DISGUISE!

IF THEY EVEN THINK WE'RE DEMONS THEY'LL BURN THE BODIES!

NOT BOTH OF US... YOU! DON'T WORRY ABOUT ME!

BUT...

...BOTH OF THEM!

WHAT I MEAN IS, WE WANT YOUR HELP MORE THAN WE WANT REVENGE.

OH YEAH?

AWK!

DON'T RELAX TOO MUCH THOUGH— IT WAS A TOUGH CHOICE!

SKREEK!

I... I SEE. WELL, WHAT CAN I DO FOR YOU?

C'MON, FRUMPLE... JUST HONOR OUR DEAL! YOU'VE GOT TO ADMIT WE LAID ONE DEVA OF A FALSE TRAIL FOR YOUR TWO FUGITIVES!

NOW IT'S YOUR TURN! JUST RESTORE MY POWERS, AND WE'LL BE OFF!

I CAN'T DO THAT.

WHAT?!! NOW LOOK YOU DOUBLE-DEALER...! EITHER YOU RESTORE MY POWERS OR...

YOU DON'T UNDERSTAND! I DON'T MEAN I WON'T RESTORE YOUR POWERS ...I MEAN I CAN'T!

I DON'T KNOW WHAT GARKIN DID TO YOU, OR HOW TO REVERSE IT. THAT'S WHY I SET YOU UP! I DIDN'T THINK YOU'D BELIEVE ME.

I'M SORRY, I REALLY AM, AND I KNOW YOU'LL PROBABLY KILL ME... BUT I CAN'T HELP YOU.

YOU CAN'T RESTORE MY POWERS.

DOES THIS MEAN WE CAN KILL HIM AFTER ALL?

YOU'RE A RATHER VICIOUS CHILD. SO WHAT'S A *PERVECT* DOING TRAVELING WITH A *KLAHD* ANYWAY?

WHO'S A CLOD?!!

ZOK!

HACK -AK -AK!

EASY KID. NOTHING PERSONAL. *EVERYONE* WHO'S A NATIVE TO THIS DIMENSION IS A *KLAHD*. KLAH... KLAHDS. GET IT?

WELL I DON'T LIKE IT.

GLAF!! HURP! HRUP!

RELAX, KID. WHAT'S IN A NAME?

THEN IT DOESN'T MATTER WHETHER PEOPLE CALL YOU PER*VERT* OR PER*VECT*?

SHADDAP.

BLOORK! GORK·GORK·GOR-

VORP

UHHH... KID?

OH... RIGHT.

CRASH!

LOOK. IF YOU'RE GOING TO ARGUE, COULD YOU *PLEASE* DO IT OUTSIDE?

YAAAAAAAAAAAAAGG!!

CAN WE KILL HIM *AAHZ*?

EASE UP, KID. JUST BECAUSE HE CAN'T RESTORE MY POWERS DOESN'T MEAN HE'S *TOTALLY* USELESS!

OH, *DEFINITELY!*
— *ANYTHING* TO MAKE UP FOR THE INCONVENIENCE!

INCONVENIENCE?

HEY KID, C'MERE!

GENTLEMEN... I COULD PROBABLY HELP YOU BETTER IF I KNEW WHAT YOU WANTED.

I'M SURE HE'D BE *MORE* THAN HAPPY TO HELP US, PARTICULARLY AFTER HE FAILED TO PAY UP ON OUR LAST DEAL...

...RIGHT, *FRUMPLE?*

CHILL OUT, KID. WELL, *FRUMPLE*, YOU CAN START BY RETURNING OUR STUFF.

AK... BIG CHEST... AGAINST... ...WALL...

I'LL CHECK IT OUT.

OUR THINGS...?

— AND A LOT MORE INTERESTING STUFF BESIDES.

TRUE ENOUGH, *FRUMPLE*. IT OCCURS TO ME THAT WE HAVEN'T BEEN ENTIRELY OPEN WITH YOU. THAT WILL HAVE TO BE CORRECTED IF WE ARE TO BECOME ALLIES.

ALLIES?!! HE TRIED TO *KILL* US AND YOU WANT TO *TRUST* HIM?!

98

WELL YOU'D BETTER CONCERN YOURSELF *THIS* TIME. YOU DON'T SEEM TO UNDERSTAND. *ISSTVAN* IS *STARTING* WITH THIS DIMENSION— HE'S OUT TO GET A MONOPOLY ON *KLAH'S* ENERGIES TO USE ON *OTHER* DIMENSIONS.

TO DO THAT, HE'LL KILL *ANYBODY* ELSE IN THIS DIMENSION WHO KNOWS HOW TO TAP THOSE ENERGIES: HE'S NOT *BIG* ON *SHARING.*

HMMM. INTERESTING THEORY, BUT WHERE'S THE PROOF? WHO'S HE KILLED?

GARKIN, FOR ONE.

THAT'S RIGHT— YOU WANTED TO KNOW WHY WE'RE TRAVELLING TOGETHER. *SKEEVE* HERE WAS *GARKIN'S* APPRENTICE BEFORE *ISSTVAN'S* ASSASSINS GOT TO HIM.

GARKIN'S APPRENTICE! NO WONDER YOU SURVIVED!

SAY... WAITAMINUTE... ASSASSINS?

THEY WOULDN'T'VE BEEN THE TWO I TELEPORTED THE OTHER DAY, WOULD THEY?

THAT'S RIGHT, AND HERE'S THE KICKER...

HE'S ARMING THEM WITH OFF-DIMENSION WEAPONS. LOOK AT THIS QUARREL.

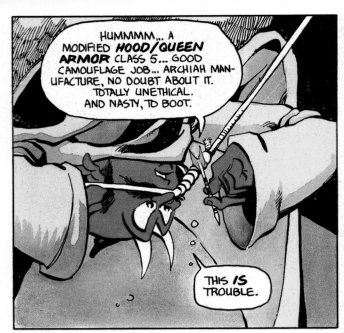

HUMMMM... A MODIFIED **HOOD/QUEEN ARMOR** CLASS 5... GOOD CAMOUFLAGE JOB... ARCHIAH MANUFACTURE, NO DOUBT ABOUT IT. TOTALLY UNETHICAL. AND NASTY, TO BOOT.

THIS **IS** TROUBLE.

NOW DO YOU SEE WHY ENLISTING YOUR AID TAKES PRIORITY OVER THE PLEASURE OF STRETCHING YOUR NECK?

I SEE YOUR POINT... **GARKIN**, EH? MOST CONVINCING. BUT WHAT CAN I DO?

YOU TELL US. **DEVEELS** ARE SUPPOSED TO HAVE WONDERS FOR EVERY OCCASION. WHAT'VE YOU GOT THAT'LL GIVE US THE EDGE OVER A MADMAN THAT KNOWS HIS MAGIK?

UM... I CAN'T THINK OF ANYTHING JUST OFF HAND. I HAVEN'T BEEN STOCKING WEAPONS LATELY... NO CALL FOR THEM IN THIS DIMENSION.

TERRIFIC.

CAN WE KILL HIM NOW, **AAHZ**?

SAY, COULD YOU PUT A MUZZLE ON HIM? WHAT **IS** YOUR PROBLEM ANYWAY?

I DON'T TAKE WELL TO BEING STRUNG UP!

POP

CRASH!

OH THAT? YOU'LL GET USED TO IT IF YOU KEEP PRACTICING MAGIK.

IT'S BEING BURNED THAT'S REALLY A PAIN.

BURNED! THAT'S IT! I CAN SEND YOU TO THE BAZAAR!

THE BAZAAR?

THE BAZAAR ON DEVA! IF YOU CAN'T FIND IT THERE, IT DOESN'T EXIST! WHY DIDN'T I THINK OF THAT BEFORE?!

NOW, I KNOW YOU'RE IN A HURRY, SO I'LL JUST GET YOU STARTED...

NOT SO FAST, FRUMPLE, WE WANT A GUARANTEE THAT THIS'LL BE A ROUND-TRIP YOU'RE SENDING US ON.

WHY, MY DEAR AAHZ, WHATEVER DO YOU MEAN?

SIMPLE -- YOU TRIED TO GET RID OF US ONCE. AND DESPITE EVERYTHING WE'VE TOLD YOU, YOU MIGHT BE TEMPTED TO SHUNT US OFF TO SOME BACKWATER DIMENSION WITH NO WAY TO GET BACK.

I GET THE IDEA. GOOD ENOUGH?

WHAT'S A D-HOPPER, *AAHZ*?

AN EXAMPLE OF *PRIMEWORLD* TECHNOLOGY, APPRENTICE.

DEPENDING ON WHICH DIMENSION YOU WANT TO GO TO, YOU JUST ALIGN THESE SYMBOLS AND PUSH THE BUTTON.

C'MON, KID, LET'S GO.

HEY!! NOT SO FAST!

WE HAVEN'T SETTLED ON A PRICE FOR THAT YET!

PRICE?!!

YOU *DO* STILL OWE US FROM OUR *LAST* DEAL.

TRUE, BUT AS YOU POINTED OUT, D-HOPPERS ARE RARE, REAL COLLECTORS ITEMS! IT'S ONLY FAIR WE RENEGOTIATE.

FRUMPLE, WE'RE IN A HURRY. I'LL TELL YOU WHAT WE'RE WILLING TO RELINQUISH ABOVE AND BEYOND OUR ORIGINAL DEAL, AND YOU CAN TAKE IT OR LEAVE IT, OKAY?

LET'S HEAR IT!

YOUR LIFE.

OH.

UMM, YES, THAT SHOULD, AH, BE AN ACCEPTABLE PRICE.

I'M SURPRIZED AT YOU, *FRUMPLE*, LETTING A COLLECTOR'S ITEM GO SO CHEAPLY.

C'MON, KID, LET'S GET MOVING.

THE
STORY
CONTINUES
IN
myth
ADVENTURES
two

Afterwords

August 3rd: Kay Reynolds called today. She tells me **Myth Adventures One** is ready to go to print—if I get the Afterwords in. "Bob's turned in his Introduction, all the color has been separated, the copyright's been here for months. Where is *your* material, Foglio?" Could tell she was ignoring the sound of things breaking, the vague animal snarls she must have heard over the phone from my end. Gnu knows I was screaming loud enough to be heard in Seattle, much less Norfolk, Virginia. I'll have to remember this: editors are made of sterner stuff than I imagined. That's a scary thought. Oh well, I'll just have to come up with something else for next time—something *better*. Hee, hee!

"What do you want me to write about?" I asked.

"Tell them how you create a chapter of **Myth Adventures**," she said.

"I don't *know* how I create a chapter of **Myth Adventures**!"

"Get something in the mail—tomorrow," she said.

"But. . . ."

"Just do it!"

"Do I get paid for this?" I asked.

At that point, the Accountant-O-Matic Phone Monitor™ on the publishers' line cut the connection. Well, maybe she'd go for the production diary. I looked it over. Decided she'd *have* to go for the production diary.

Production Schedule Diary
Myth Adventures—Chapter 4

June 3rd: Time to start another chapter of **MA**. This chapter will cover the chase through the town, leaning on Frumple and arriving at the Bazaar. I've got to get the pencils to Rich by June 21st. No problem. Begin layout today.

June 4th: It can't be done! I give up. This chapter is about as funny as a broken crutch! Even massive rereadings of old *Jerry Lewis* comics have produced no effect, no inspiration. I've lost it. Burned-out at 28. Mother was right: should have taken over family alligator farm when I had the chance. Now it's gone. All gone. . . .

June 5th: Doomed! Rich is gonna string me up. Bob is gonna have my hide. Kay will eviscerate me. The end is near.

June 6th: I AM IN CONTROL! I AM ARTIST—THEY ARE CHARACTERS ON PAPER. MUST MAKE FUNNY. HOW? THINK FUNNY. LIVE FUNNY. EAT FUNNY. WHEN EAT LAST? WHAT DAY IS THIS? NOT IMPORTANT. DISREGARD. EAT! EAT FUNNY!

June 7 (?): Better. Five boxes of tapioca (must remember to cook next time) have done the trick! Have them torture Frumple while talking to him in shop. Big yocks there. Remember to ask Kay about bondage market.

June 8th: Preliminary layout finished! Chapter is supposed to be 26 pages. It's only 25! Maybe I can throw in more running around and screaming. **I** do it. Why shouldn't they?

June 9th: Buy paper. Call Rich and ask when I'll get free paper. Phone cuts off. Does *everybody* have one of those damn things?

June 10th: Walk around neighborhood for last time. Activate timelocks on door and begin work. Find reference for town in old *National Geographic*. Quaint town of Baveriphlact in Urals. Four pages finished.

June 11th: Four more pages finished. I hate crowds. No crowds in photos of Baveriphlact.

June 12th: Four **more** pages. What am I doing? This isn't what I laid out! What are they saying! Bob's characters are taking over—**again!** Help me!

June 13th: Losing it. Entering fugue state. Hell with script. Go with it!

June 14th: Must go back and fix Aahz at chapter opening. He's beginning to look like a meatloaf with teeth.

June 15th: Who wrote *that*?! What's going on here?

June 16th: Pages—yes—more pages! Baveriphlact—nice station. Finished.

June 17th: Must turn in work to Rich. Due to roadwork on driveway at Elf Manor, have to walk up from gatehouse. Hope wolves are fed. Carstairs tells me Rich is in basement office. Will never get used to an entire domestic staff all under four feet tall with pointed ears. Cosmetic surgery, perhaps? Fans? Oh well, Rich goes over the book. Rich talks about going to 3-D holography sometime next year. Sounds interesting. He hands me my check and has Mike fly me back in the Elf Copter. Nice.

Ask Mike to drop me off somewhere I can cash check. Drops me off at bank. Should have asked him to land first. Hospital okay. Food's lousy, but nurses are cute and so attentive. I love the comics biz!

Phil Foglio
Chicago, Illinois
August, 1985